# ToyTales

*For Matilda*
*A.E.*
*For Cass and Roy Smith*
*S.G.*

ORCHARD BOOKS
96 Leonard Street, London, EC2A 4XD
Orchard Books Australia
14 Mars Road, Lane Cove, NSW 2066
ISBN 1 86039 020 X (hardback)
ISBN 1 84121 081 1 (paperback)
First published in Great Britain in 1996
This edition published in 1999
Text © Sally Grindley 1996
Illustrations © Andy Ellis 1996
The rights of Sally Grindley to be identified as the author and Andy Ellis to be
identified as the illustrator of this Work have been asserted by them in
accordance with the Copyright, Designs and Patents Act 1988.
A CIP catalogue record for this book is available from the British Library.
Printed in Dubai

# Toy Tales

Written by Sally Grindley

Illustrated by Andy Ellis

ORCHARD BOOKS

# Contents

# The New Arrival

When Tom and Sarah were born, the toys began to arrive. First of all there were cuddly toys: pink teddies with squeaky tummies, blue rabbits with bendy bodies and rainbow coloured clowns with bells inside. And there were plastic things, like bricks and rings and rattles, which real toys say aren't 'proper' toys at all.

As Tom and Sarah grew, so did the collection of toys. Pull-along Hen came when they were two.

They pulled her along so fast that she would trip over and bounce on her head – OUCH! That made her very grumpy, especially when her paint began to chip.

Little Blue Train came when the twins were three. They loved him and pushed him round his track for hours and hours – CHOO CHOO! – until he was quite giddy – OOCH OOCH!

Elephant Mum and Elephant Small arrived soon afterwards. At first they cuddled up in Sarah's bed every night. It was nice and warm but Elephant Small kept falling out – WAAAH!

As Christmases and birthdays came and went, more
and more toys arrived to clutter up the playroom.
Adventure Man, Rag Doll, Jack-in-the-Box, Plastic
Penguin and Scaredy Cat were all Christmas presents.
Cling-on Duck, Bean Bag Frog, Silver Seaplane,
Big Yellow Crane were birthday presents, and
Two Ton Ted had been won at a funfair.

    Then one day there was a new arrival.
It was huge, it was square and it stood
right in the middle of the playroom.

    "What's that there for?"
said Little Blue Train.
"It's right by my track.
I won't be able to
go round if it
stays there."

"I'd say it's a box for putting things in," said Clockwork Mouse.

"It might have things in it already," said Rag Doll.

"Let's look," said Two Ton Ted.

He lifted the top and peered inside, but the box was completely empty.

"If it's a box for putting things in," said Two Ton Ted, "nothing's been put in it yet."

"Well, what do you suppose is going to be put in it?" said Cling-on Duck.

The toys all had a think.

"Clothes," said Rag Doll.

"Books," said Clockwork Mouse.

"Plastic things," said Silver Seaplane.

"I hope not," said Plastic Penguin.

"Oh, I didn't mean you," said Clockwork Mouse.

"It might not be for putting things *in*," said Little Blue Train. "It might be for putting things *on*. It might be for sitting on."

"That's a good idea," said Two Ton Ted, and he clambered up on top. Rag Doll climbed up as well and they looked around the room from their new position.

"I can see out of the window," said Two Ton Ted.

"If that's not a box for putting things in," said Rag Doll, "why has it got all that empty space inside?"

"That's a jolly good point," said Adventure Man. "Just what I was thinking."

"Why don't *we* get in?" said Cling-on Duck. "It could be our home."

"Wowee, yes!" cried Rag Doll.

"No fear," said Scaredy Cat. "It'll be dark inside."

"Not if we leave the top open," said Little Blue Train. "But we'll have to move it right out of the way of my track."

Two Ton Ted and Elephant Mum leant against the
box and pushed and pushed – HEAVE! – until the box
was right up against the wall.  Then toys from all over
the playroom ran and slid and chugged and rolled
across the floor, chattering excitedly.  Those who could
climbed up the sides of the box and jumped in.
Big Yellow Crane and Two Ton Ted helped the
others, until the playroom was empty
apart from the bookshelf
and a trolley full of
building bricks.

"I'll sit outside and guard you," said Two Ton Ted.

"I'll stay outside and help you in and out," said Big Yellow Crane.

From inside the box came giggles and squeals as the toys made themselves comfortable.  Then one by one they fell asleep, and all that could be heard was Elephant Mum snoring.

In the morning Tom and Sarah went upstairs to put all the toys into their new toybox.  Imagine how surprised they were to find it had already been done!

# Two Ton Ted's Story

Two Ton Ted was a funfair bear. Sarah had won him by rolling a coin onto a lucky number. Two Ton Ted was happy living with Tom and Sarah and all the other toys, but sometimes he missed the lights and the noise and the colour of the funfair, and he missed his best friend, Blue Bow Bear.

One day, Tom stuck a poster on the playroom wall. It read GIANT FUNFAIR and said that the funfair would be visiting the town at the weekend.

# • Two Ton Ted's Story •

Two Ton Ted's tummy went all funny.
He tried not to look at the poster.
He tried to forget what it said.
But the poster stared at him
with it's spinning carousel,
and he couldn't help staring
back and feeling all excited.

On Saturday night, as soon as everyone was asleep,
Two Ton Ted slipped out of the playroom and down
the stairs. He opened a window and climbed through,
into the pouring rain, then he listened hard. He could
hear the sounds of the funfair jumbling through
the night air. He ran towards them
as fast as he could, splashing
along the empty
pavements.

The sounds grew louder and louder. Suddenly, there in front of him sprawled the roundabouts, the big wheel, the bumper cars, the coconut shy, the rifle range and so many other sideshows. Two Ton Ted's eyes grew wider and wider with excitement. Here were the lights and the noise and the colour. Here was the world he had left behind a year ago.

Two Ton Ted crept round the outside of the fairground so that no-one would see him, then he made himself as thin as he could – which wasn't very

thin – and
squeezed
between
two trucks
to find himself
in amongst the stalls.
He pretended to belong
to one of the stalls while he looked around, but a
rough voice said, "'Ere, go and find your own stall!"

Two Ton Ted looked up to see a huge green frog
staring at him crossly.

"Sorry," said Two Ton Ted, "but can you tell me
where the ROLL A LUCKY NUMBER stall is."

"Over there, mate," said the frog. "Now push off."

Two Ton Ted trod his way carefully
over the muddy ground. He was
a very cold, very wet, very
grubby bear by now, and
his paws were sore
because people kept
treading on them.

Then he saw it – the ROLL A LUCKY NUMBER stall. He looked at the great big bears hanging from the top of the stall. Other bears sat in the middle, where a man was yelling, "Last chance to win a bear!"

One of the hanging bears saw Two Ton Ted and shook his fist at him.

"Go away," he said. "We're the next to be chosen when someone wins. You dare push in!"

But then another voice whispered excitedly, "Hey, Two Ton Ted! Over here. It's me, Blue Bow Bear."

Two Ton Ted moved closer to the stall, and there was his friend, Blue Bow Bear, waving at him.

"I missed the funfair," said Two Ton Ted.

"Huh!" moaned the big bear. "You don't know when you are well off. We hang here all day, hoping that someone nice will win us and take us to a cosy new home where we will be loved."

"He's right, you know," said Blue Bow Bear. "You remember the lights and the noise and the colour, but you've forgotten the bad bits."

At that moment, the man in the middle of the stall dragged out an enormous box and began to pull down the hanging bears and throw them into it for the night.

"Quick! Run away before he catches you," yelled the big bear, as the man tugged at his leg and hurled him across the stall and into the box.

"You're right," said Two Ton Ted to Blue Bow Bear. "I don't want to come back. But you could come with me!"

"Oh, please take me with you!" cried Blue Bow Bear.

Even as she spoke, a rough hand grabbed Two Ton Ted's ear and lifted him up.

" 'Ere where did you come from? Into the box."

Two Ton Ted wriggled and kicked and tried to free himself, but the man held him tight. Then Blue Bow Bear pushed the man's tin of money onto the floor and the noise made him lose his grip for a second. Two Ton Ted twisted himself free, grabbed Blue Bow Bear's paw, leapt down from the table, and they ran away as fast as they could.

They ran and ran, splashing along the empty pavements, until at last they reached the house. They clambered through the window and crept back to the playroom. The other toys were delighted to see Two Ton Ted, and to meet Blue Bow Bear, and they listened in amazement as he told them all about his adventures.

Two Ton Ted looked at the poster saying GIANT FUNFAIR, but this time his tummy didn't go funny. Funfairs were all right, but home was best. He hugged Blue Bow Bear and they settled down to sleep.

Next morning, Mum found muddy paw marks all round the window. And to this day, no-one has ever discovered where Blue Bow Bear appeared from.

# Little Blue Train's Story

Little Blue Train was bored.

"I'm bored," he said to the toybox toys. "I never go anywhere exciting. Just round and round the same old piece of track until I'm giddy. Then round and round again backwards, if I'm lucky. I want to go somewhere else. I want to go exploring."

And that's exactly what he decided to do. When midnight came, one bright, moonlit night, he leapt into action.

"I'm off to see the world," he said. "Who's coming with me? It's a train's job to carry passengers to all sorts of faraway places."

The toybox immediately came to life with great shouts of excitement.

"I'm coming," said Bean Bag Frog. "I might find a pond somewhere."

Big Yellow Crane helped to lower Little Blue Train out of the toybox.

"Oooo!" said Scaredy Cat in her high, squeaky voice. "It's very naughty to leave the toybox without permission."

"Who says?" said Rag Doll, climbing out of the toybox and into one of Little Blue Train's carriages. "As long as we're all back here by morning, no-one will ever know."

27

"What if you don't get back by morning, that's what I want to know?" said Adventure Man. "Much too risky, if you ask me."

"We don't care," said Cling-on Duck, clinging on to Bean Bag Frog's arm. "We're going."

Little Blue Train blew his whistle and started up his engine. "Anyone else for a tour of the world?" he called excitedly.

More toys clambered into the empty seats. Scaredy Cat tutted and Adventure Man said it would be their own fault if anything happened to them. But nothing could stop them.

Little Blue Train couldn't believe how good it felt.

Now he could go in whatever direction he chose.
He puffed his way round the playroom first
of all, not just round the little bit in the
middle, which is where he was
usually put, but right round
the outside. He came
across a petrol station
and stopped at the
pumps to ask
for petrol,

just for
the fun of it.
He went past a
sailing ship made
of bricks and blew his
whistle at the pirates who
were climbing the mast.  He
chugged up to Two Ton Ted, who
was sat in the corner on his own, so that
all his passengers could wave and shout hello.

Then Rag Doll and Bean Bag Frog shouted, "We want to go out of the room! We want to go out of the room!"

Little Blue Train could feel the excitement running through his wheels. The door was open and he headed for the gap as fast as he could, whistling loudly, then he was through it and out on to the landing. He had never been there before. He turned on his lights so that he could see better and went in the direction of another open door. Rag Doll yelled, "This is Tom and Sarah's room! I've been in here before. Go under the bed, go under the bed!"

The passengers squealed with fright as Little Blue

Train pushed under the hanging bedclothes and they
entered the long, dark tunnel. Bean Bag Frog said it
was like being on a ghost train. Cling-on Duck clung
on even more tightly to his arm when they passed
Tom's slippers with their cat faces, whose eyes lit up in
Little Blue Train's headlights. Then they were out
again, and back through the door on to the landing.

"Let's go downstairs!" Rag Doll shouted excitedly.

"Downstairs! Downstairs!" shouted the other toys,
and Little Blue Train headed for the top. When he
looked down he gasped in fright. He had never seen
stairs before and it was a very long way to the bottom.

"Are you sure?" he asked nervously. "We could try another room."

"Downstairs! Downstairs!" the toys shouted again.

Little Blue Train moved gingerly to the edge of the top step, took a deep breath and pushed forward. Suddenly he could feel his wheels going from underneath him and he seemed to be flying and twisting in the air and bouncing on the ground and flying again and bouncing – OUCH! He closed his eyes and then – CRASH! – they landed in a tangled heap.

For a moment all was quiet. Then, one after the other, the toys began to clamber out.

Luckily, the carpet was soft and no-one was hurt.

Rag Doll said, "That *was* fun!"

Some of the toys weren't so sure. Little Blue Train lay twisted where he had fallen. Rag Doll and Bean Bag Frog helped to straighten him up.

"We'll have to stay here for the rest of the night, I'm afraid," said Little Blue Train. "Coming down stairs is one thing, climbing back up them is quite another."

"Perhaps we had better stick to upstairs from now on," said Cling-on Duck. "But that was fun, wasn't it?"

So the toys settled down to sleep on the deep, soft carpet at the bottom of the stairs. And that's where Tom and Sarah found them in the morning.

# Elephant Small's Story

Elephant Small was where he shouldn't have been.
Where he should have been was in the toybox. At
the end of every day, he and Elephant Mum were
put back in the toybox together. That's where they
always slept, trunks wrapped round each other, until
the sounds of the morning woke them once again.
But tonight was different. Elephant Mum was
safely tucked up in the toybox as usual. Elephant
Small wasn't.

Elephant Small was in the garden shed. He had been there since teatime, when Sarah had run indoors and forgotten all about him.

"Let me out! I want my mummy!" he had yelled over and over again, but there was no-one to hear. It hadn't been too bad at first while it was still light. He had had fun tipping over flowerpots and watching the spiders and woodlice scuttle away from underneath them. He had found an old ball and kicked that around, shooting goals into the grass collector of the lawnmower. But now he stood on the lawnmower and looked out through the little window.

It was getting dark
and he had never been
in the dark without
Elephant Mum.

It was getting cold
and he wanted to feel
Elephant Mum's great big
body snuggled up alongside him.
"I want my mummy!" he wailed.
Elephant Small decided that he would
have to escape through the window. He
picked up a large flowerpot and threw it at
the window as hard as he could. CRASH!
The window shattered into hundreds
of pieces. Now he clambered on to
the lawnmower again and tried
to jump from the handles
on to the window frame.

Three times he tried, and three times he landed – BUMP! – on the shed floor. The fourth time he took a deep breath, squatted down and then leapt – W-H-E-E-E ! – and managed to grab the window sill. He hung there for a moment, then heaved himself up and stood looking at the ground outside. He closed his eyes tight and jumped – THUMP! – OUCH! – on to the path below.

"I'm out!" he gasped excitedly.

But suddenly he felt very scared. The garden was dark, the garden was full of sounds, the garden moved with strange shadows.

"I'm scared," whimpered Elephant Small. "I want my mummy!"

There was a loud thump behind him and

Elephant Small spun round in fright. He found
himself face to face with a large rabbit, not a toybox
rabbit, but a real rabbit with a nose that twitched
and ears that flapped.

"What sort of a thing are you?" asked the rabbit.

"I'm an elephant," said Elephant Small nervously.

"Rubbish," said the rabbit. "You're not big enough
and your skin's all fluffy. I've heard about elephants
from my grandpa. They're great big animals and
they've got tough wrinkly skin."

"Well, I'm a toy elephant," said Elephant Small.
"And we come in all sizes and colours and fluffs."

"Why were you crying?" asked the rabbit.

"I want my mummy," said Elephant Small, and he began to cry again.

"Well, where is she?" asked the rabbit.

"She's all tucked up in the toybox upstairs in that house over there."

"You mean you live inside a house?" asked the rabbit, who couldn't believe his big floppy ears. "I'm glad I'm real. Much better to run around a garden."

"I don't like it one bit," said Elephant Small. "It's cold and it's dark and there are funny noises and I'm scared and I want to go home."

"Come on then," said the rabbit. "I'll take you. But I won't go too close to the house. That's a dangerous place for real animals."

Elephant Small and the rabbit set off down the path. Elephant Small kept as close to the rabbit as he could. When an owl swooped down low – T-O-O-W-H-I-T! – T-O-O-W-H-O-O!  Elephant Small was so frightened he threw himself at the rabbit and pushed him off the path into the flowers.

"S-s-s-sorry," said Elephant Small as he helped the rabbit to his feet.

But the rabbit said, "Don't say sorry, funny elephant thing.  You just saved my life.  That owl might have eaten me."

"Wow!" said Elephant Small.  "I told you my toybox was better.  Nobody tries to eat you there!"

Elephant Small and the rabbit carried on along the garden path, until Elephant Small looked up and suddenly started jumping up and down in excitement.

"It's my mummy, it's my mummy! Up there at the window."

The rabbit looked up and saw a window full of different shaped heads bobbing around, and then the window opened and they all started calling at once.

"Where have you been Elephant Small? We've been looking for you everywhere?" shouted Two Ton Ted.

"Thank goodness you're safe," said Elephant Mum. "Now come back inside to me."

But that presented a problem. Elephant Mum was upstairs in the house, Elephant Small was downstairs in the garden, and the door was firmly bolted.

"My rope might do the trick," said Adventure Man. "We can throw it down to him."

But the rope wasn't long enough.

"I've got an idea," said Rag Doll, and she disappeared back inside the playroom.

Elephant Mum said, "Don't worry, dear, we'll save you."

Rag Doll soon came back and Two Ton Ted helped her to throw down a rope made from his braces, Adventure Man's rope, Rag Doll's ribbons, Pull-along Hen's string, and a brightly coloured mish-mash of anything else they could find.

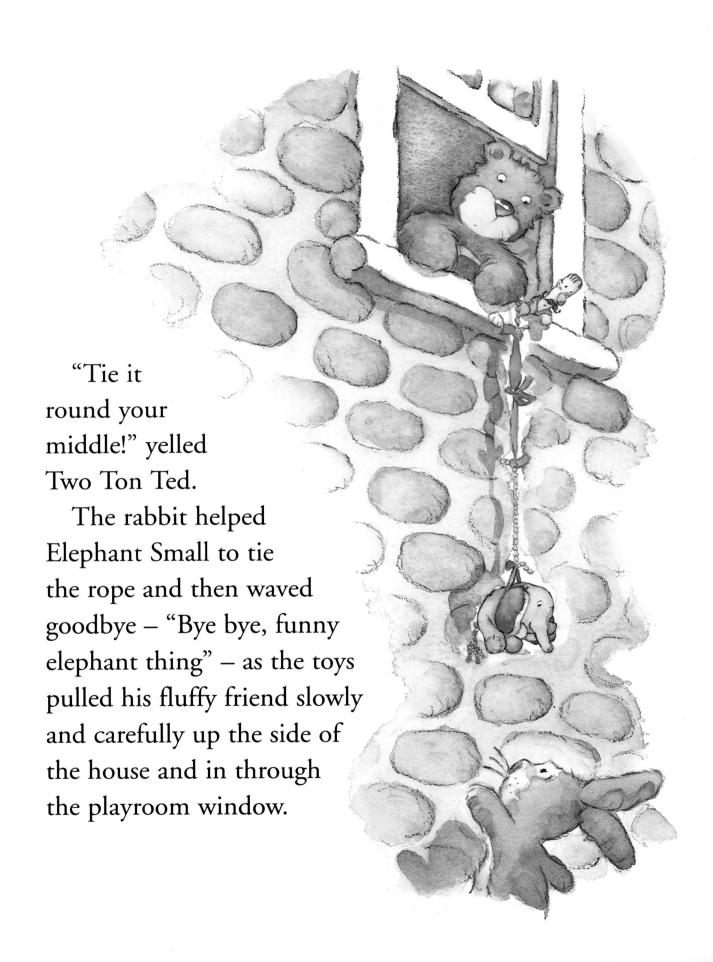

"Tie it round your middle!" yelled Two Ton Ted.

The rabbit helped Elephant Small to tie the rope and then waved goodbye – "Bye bye, funny elephant thing" – as the toys pulled his fluffy friend slowly and carefully up the side of the house and in through the playroom window.

Elephant Small told his friends all about his adventures, but he was very glad to be back in the toybox. Then, yawning loudly, he wrapped his trunk round Elephant Mum, she wrapped her trunk round him, and they settled down to sleep.

# Silver Seaplane's Story

Tom and Sarah were going on a picnic. They rummaged in the toybox to find some toys to take with them.

"Take me, take me!" little voices cried from every corner, but of course Tom and Sarah couldn't hear them.

The lucky ones to be chosen were Cling-on Duck, Adventure Man, Rag Doll and Silver Seaplane.

"Have a good time," said Two Ton Ted.

"I wish I was going," said Pull-along Hen.

"Ooooh, I don't!" said Scaredy Cat in her high, squeaky voice.

"They might get lost. They might have an accident. It's much safer here in our box."

"It's also very boring sometimes," said Rag Doll.

During the car journey Cling-on Duck clung on to Sarah's jacket. Tom played with Adventure Man and twisted his arms and legs around so much that Adventure Man felt quite exhausted. Rag Doll and Silver Seaplane sat excitedly on the back shelf. They couldn't wait to reach the picnic spot.

At last they came to the side of a lake and stopped.

Mum and Dad put a blanket on the grass and unloaded the picnic hamper. Tom and Sarah laid the toys on the blanket, but they didn't play with them. They ate their food and then went off for a walk with Mum and Dad, leaving the toys behind.

"Let's have some fun!" said Silver Seaplane. "Let's fly over the lake and land on that island in the middle. We can go exploring while Tom and Sarah are away."

"I don't think we should," said Adventure Man.

"Course we should," said Rag Doll. "Where's your sense of adventure?"

"I haven't got one," said Adventure Man. "I was made without one."

"I'm going," said Cling-on Duck. She clambered over Silver Seaplane and clung on to the side of the window. Rag Doll sat on top and held on as tightly as possible.

"Are you coming or not?" said Silver Seaplane to Adventure Man.

"I'm staying here," said Adventure Man. "Just be careful all of you."

"Off we go then," said Silver Seaplane.

He started his engines up – BRRM, BRRRM, BRRRRM – and began to move across the grass. One more very loud BRRRRMMMM and suddenly they were up in the air, up, up, and flying over the lake.

Silver Seaplane flew round and round the lake, and then made for the island in the middle. He dropped down on to the water and skied across to the shore. Rag Doll and Cling-on Duck climbed out.

"Come on," they said, "Let's go and see what we can find."

They set off into the tall reeds that grew everywhere, while Silver Seaplane chugged happily round the outside of the island.

They watched grasshoppers leaping from one stalk of grass to another. They sniffed flowers and sneezed on the pollen. Then Cling-on Duck said that she wanted to see what a real duck's nest was like.

They looked and looked until at last they found a nest. Cling-on Duck waddled into it, shuffled around and then sat there just for a few moments, dreaming about what it would be like to be a real duck.

But she sat there for a few moments too long. Suddenly a real duck flew in, grabbed her in its beak, flew off again, and dropped her right in the middle of the lake – SPLASH!

Rag Doll was horrified. She ran as fast as she could to find Silver Seaplane. Cling-on Duck spluttered around in the middle of the lake and yelled, "Help! Help! I can't swim!"

Adventure Man heard her. Adventure Man saw her. He ran to the edge of the lake and leapt in, fully clothed, and swam and swam and swam until he reached his struggling friend.

Cling-on Duck clung on to Adventure Man's arm and buried her head in his neck.

"Oh, thank you, thank you," she sobbed.

Then they heard the sound of an engine, and there was Silver Seaplane gliding towards them.

"You're a hero, Adventure Man!" yelled Rag Doll who was sitting on top. "You deserve a medal."

Adventure Man blushed bright red as he carefully lifted Cling-on Duck on board. Then he jumped proudly into the front seat. Rag Doll hugged Cling-on Duck until Silver Seaplane reached the picnic blanket.

Luckily, Mum, Dad, Tom and Sarah were still out walking, so the toys settled down in the sun to dry. They were still quite damp when Tom and Sarah came back. Tom and Sarah couldn't understand why.

# Rag Doll's Story

Rag Doll wanted something different to wear. She had been dressed in the same old clothes since she was made, and she thought it was time she had new ones.

"Some trousers would make a change," she said to Elephant Mum. "Or a jacket with spots or stripes. I'm fed up with all these silly frills and flowers."

"But where will you get them from, dear?" asked Elephant Mum.

Rag Doll had no idea.  Tom and Sarah didn't seem to have noticed that her clothes were becoming very shabby.  And she knew that if she began to look too old, Tom and Sarah's mother might give her away to a jumble sale.

"Have you thought about looking in the attic?" said Elephant Mum.  "I've read

in stories that people often keep chests full of clothes in their attics."

"What's an attic?" asked Rag Doll.

"Why, it's the space under the roof and above the ceiling," said Elephant Mum.  "You have to climb a ladder to reach it though, dear.  It might be a bit dangerous for you."

Rag Doll didn't care.  She wasn't scared, and if it meant she could have some new clothes, she would try anything.  Rag Doll went to see Two Ton Ted and Blue Bow Bear to ask if they would help.

That night, when everyone was asleep, Rag Doll, Two Ton Ted and Blue Bow Bear crept into the hall. They opened a cupboard where the ladder was kept and pulled and heaved – WHOAAA! – until they had it in place underneath the door to the attic. Rag Doll began to climb. Two Ton Ted held the bottom of the ladder to keep it steady.

"I'm going too," said Blue Bow Bear. "I might find a new bow."

She stepped onto the ladder and it rocked wildly.

"AHHHH! Be careful!" cried Rag Doll, holding on to the ladder tightly to stop herself from falling.

When she reached the top, she stood on tiptoe and Blue Bow Bear held her legs. Rag Doll pushed upwards as hard as she could against the attic door. It flew open. She grabbed hold of the door frame and pulled herself up through it, then she held out her hand to help Blue Bow Bear.

The toys turned on the light and looked around. There were tins and baskets and boxes and bags and drawers and shelves all higgledy-piggledy everywhere.

"Wow!" said Rag Doll. "We've found treasure!"

"Let's explore," said Blue Bow Bear.

They opened lids, emptied
baskets, dug around in bags,
pulled out drawers and
clambered on shelves.  They
found old photographs, books
and paintings and a large mirror.
They found a guitar with only two strings and a rusty
xylophone.  They pretended to
be in a band and practised in
front of the mirror –
TWANG! TING!
They found a rocking horse
and rocked backwards and
forwards on it, pretending to be
cowgirls – YEE HA!  And then they
found a wooden chest.  They opened it carefully.
Inside was a pile of
baby's clothes.

"Look at these!" said Rag
Doll excitedly.  "Come
on, let's try some on."

For the next hour they dressed themselves up in different clothes and paraded in front of the mirror. Rag Doll's favourites were a tiny pair of shoes, a pair of stripy trousers and a bright yellow jumper. Blue Bow Bear searched and searched but she couldn't find any bows. But she did find a pair of blue pyjamas with a picture of a bear on them.

"Pyjamas!" she cried. "I've always wanted pyjamas! How do I look?"

"Great," said Rag Doll. "How do I look?"

"Perfect," said Blue Bow Bear.

They were about to try something else, when a tiny voice cried, "Do you think you could help me out?"

"Did you hear something?" said Rag Doll.

"I heard a voice," said Blue Bow Bear. "It came from over there."

The two toys tiptoed across the attic to where they thought the voice had come from.

"Please help me out," said the voice again.

In the corner was a dirty old brown box. Rag Doll carefully lifted the lid. Something moved underneath a pile of papers. Then a head popped up, and out crawled a battered old tin soldier.

"At last," said Tin Soldier. "Thought I was going to be stuck in that box for ever."

"How long have you been in there?" asked Rag Doll.

"Years," said Tin Soldier. "Ever since George stopped playing with me."

"George? You mean Sarah and Tom's father?" said Blue Bow Bear.

"You must come and stay with us," said Rag Doll. "We live in a toybox downstairs in the playroom with lots of other toys."

"Are there any other soldiers?  Do you think we might have a battle?  I haven't had a battle for ages."

"No soldiers, I'm afraid," said Rag Doll.  "But the other toys will play with you."

Blue Bow Bear helped him out of the box and carried him to the doorway.  Then she climbed down the ladder with Tin Soldier on her back.

Two Ton Ted had fallen asleep at the foot of the ladder. Blue Bow Bear gently woke him up and the four toys made their way back to the playroom.

Tin Soldier was delighted with his new home, Rag Doll was delighted with her new clothes and Blue Bow Bear was delighted with her pyjamas. As you can imagine, Tom and Sarah's father was amazed to see his Tin Soldier again. And their mother could never understand how Rag Doll and Blue Bow Bear came to be wearing Tom and Sarah's baby clothes.

# Plastic Penguin's Story

Plastic Penguin was a bath toy. She used to stand on the edge of the bath, waiting for Tom or Sarah to plunge her into the water. When they did she would whistle – PHHOOOO! – as the hot water flooded over her. It was always a shock, because penguins aren't used to hot water, even plastic penguins, but she loved being able to swim about.

When Tom and Sarah stopped playing with her, Plastic Penguin was put into the toybox.

Sometimes they took her out just to look at her, but they never put her in the bath again and she really missed her swims.

One day Two Ton Ted shouted to all the toys, "It's snowing!  Come and look, it's snowing!"

The toys clambered out of the toybox as quickly as they could and rushed to the window.  They peered out and saw great white flakes floating past and falling to the ground.  "PHHOOOO!" whistled Plastic Penguin excitedly.  She had never seen snow before, but she knew that snow was what real penguins like more than anything else.

The other toys went back to the toybox and made themselves comfortable for the night. But Plastic Penguin watched and watched as the snow turned everything white. The garden didn't look like Tom and Sarah's garden any more. It looked like just the sort of place where even a plastic penguin would feel at home.

"Go and try it," said Two Ton Ted softly, "before it gets too dark. I'll watch out for you."

Plastic Penguin didn't need to be told twice. She waddled quietly out of the bedroom and down the stairs. She climbed through the cat flap, and there it was. Snow everywhere.

"PHHOOOO!" she whistled as she stepped into it and the snow covered her feet.

"It's cold! But it's what penguins like best."

She took a few more steps and nearly fell over. Her feet slipped and slid on the icy path – WHOOAAA!

From the bedroom window Two Ton Ted chuckled. "What's it like?" he called.

"It's cold and it's slippery and it's crunchy, and it's the most wonderful thing in the world!" shouted Plastic Penguin. "Come down!"

"No thanks," said Two Ton Ted. "I like being in the warm."

"Watch this then," said Plastic Penguin. She took a few steps, then she dropped down on to her tummy and tobogganed along the path – WHEEEEEE!  She stood up, turned round, and tobogganed back the other way – WHEEEEEEE!  The third time, she went so fast that she couldn't stop.

"Look out!" yelled Two Ton Ted, but he was too late.  Plastic Penguin whizzed off the garden path and straight into the pond – SPLASH!  Then "PHHOOO!" she whistled, as the icy water flooded over her.  It was a shock because plastic penguins aren't used to icy water.

"Are you all right?" called Two Ton Ted.

He needn't have worried.  Plastic Penguin was swimming around and having the time of her life.  Every now and again, she jumped out of the water and then plunged back in.  She swam on her front, she swam on her back, she twisted and turned and dived and leapt in the air – PHHOOOO!  And then "PHOO!" she went, and "PH–", she was tired out. She dragged herself out of the pond and lay by the side, breathing heavily and shivering in the cold.

"What's the matter?" called Two Ton Ted.

Plastic Penguin didn't have enough strength to reply. Two Ton Ted rushed from the window, ran down the stairs, clambered through the downstairs window (he was too big to crawl through the cat flap), and began to make his way across the garden. It wasn't easy. He slipped and slithered and fell head over heels. His paws grew heavier as the snow stuck to his fur. His whole body shook with the cold. He tried tobogganing on his tummy like Plastic Penguin, but he just spun round in circles. So he crawled on his paws and knees, until at last he reached his toybox friend.

"Come on, Plastic Penguin," he said. "Let's get you back in the warm."

He took hold of her flipper and tried to pull her along, but he kept falling over. So he rolled her over on to her tummy, went back down on his paws and knees, and pushed her from behind. When they reached the cat flap, Two Ton Ted lifted Plastic Penguin up and bundled her gently through the flap, then heaved himself through the window.

By now, Two Ton Ted was tired out too. He knew he wouldn't be able to pull himself and Plastic Penguin back upstairs. So he carried her to the cat's basket, and that's where they spent the night.

Tom and Sarah could never understand how two of their toys came to be in the cat's basket. As for Plastic Penguin, she decided to wait for warmer weather before she went for another swim in the pond.

# Jack-in-the-Box's Story

Jack-in-the-Box was noisy. Sometimes he was very noisy. Once, he was impossibly noisy and silly too. That's when the other toys decided to do something about it.

Jack-in-the-Box wasn't *trying* to upset everyone. He was just enjoying himself, singing and whistling and cracking bad jokes, leaping out of his box and making the other toys jump. So he couldn't see why they weren't enjoying themselves too.

He had been doing it all day.  Now it was the middle of the night, and he still hadn't stopped.

He frightened Elephant Small by jumping out at him just as he was dropping off to sleep – BOO!

"WAAH!" yelped Elephant Small.

He jumped up and banged Elephant Mum under the chin.  She smacked him with her trunk but he thought she was just playing.

He whistled so loudly at Cling-on Duck that she put her wings over her ears and fell off the toybox.

"Enough is enough," said Tin Soldier.  "An old soldier needs his sleep."

"I've got an idea," said Rag Doll, and she whispered in Elephant Mum's ear. Elephant Mum whispered to Tin Soldier, Tin Soldier whispered to Adventure Man, Adventure Man whispered to Clockwork Mouse, and so on until every toy in the toybox knew – The Plan.

Next time Jack-in-the-Box disappeared inside his box, Elephant Mum held the lid shut and sat on it. Then the other toys put The Plan into action. Two by two they climbed quietly, carefully out of the toybox. Big Yellow Crane and Two Ton Ted helped those who couldn't climb very well.

"My lid's stuck!" came Jack-in-the-Box's muffled voice. "Someone help me!"

The toys looked around the playroom and began to choose

where they would sleep.

"I'm going to station myself in that empty space on the bookshelf," said Little Blue Train. He made himself

comfortable, and some of the smaller toys clambered into his carriages.

"Let's sleep on that cushion," said Bean Bag Frog to Rag Doll, and they snuggled down.

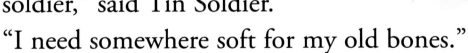

"Make room for an old soldier," said Tin Soldier. "I need somewhere soft for my old bones."

"Adventure Man doesn't need anywhere soft," said Adventure Man, and he lay down on the floor in the corner of the room.

"Let me out! I'm stuck!" came Jack-in-the-Box's voice again.

Elephant Small stood by
the toybox. "I want my
mummy," he said.

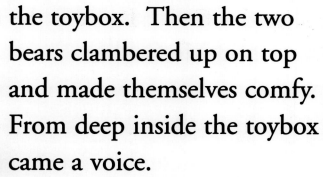

"She's coming now," said
Two Ton Ted, as he lowered
Elephant Mum to the floor.

"We'll sleep over here
behind the curtain,"
said Elephant Mum.
"Come along, dear."

"On with the top," said Two Ton Ted, and he and
Blue Bow Bear and Big Yellow Crane quickly closed

the toybox. Then the two
bears clambered up on top
and made themselves comfy.
From deep inside the toybox
came a voice.

"Oooo, I'm out at last!
Ooooooo, why is it so dark?
Has someone put the top on
the toybox? Why isn't anyone

answering me?" said Jack-in-the-Box.

He leaned right out of his box and felt around him. He couldn't feel anything. Jack-in-the-Box shuffled across the toybox and felt again. He still couldn't feel anything at all.

"Funny," he thought. "Where is everyone? Hallo-o-o. Where are you-ou?"

There was no answer. "They must be outside," he said to himself. "Why didn't they tell me they were going? I'll push the top open and have a look."

He curled up in his box as tightly as possible and then sprang up with all his might. He banged his head hard – OUCH! – and the top didn't move.

"Let me out!" yelled Jack-in-the-Box.

"No fear," said Two Ton Ted. "You're too noisy. Go to sleep like a good toy and we'll let you out in the morning."

"Let me out or I shall whistle," said Jack-in-the-Box.

"Then we won't let you out in the morning either," said Two Ton Ted.

"It's not fair," said Jack-in-the-Box. "I was only enjoying myself."

"Well, we weren't," said Two Ton Ted. "You haven't stopped annoying us all day long."

"Spoilsports," said Jack-in-the-Box.

"Go to sleep," said Two Ton Ted.

"Shan't," said Jack-in-the-Box.

For a while he made as much noise as he possibly

could. But it wasn't much fun having no-one to leap at, and it wasn't much fun having no-one to groan at his jokes, and it wasn't much fun whistling in the dark. It wasn't too long before Jack-in-the-Box mumbled one last "It's not fair", and then all was quiet.

"At last!" murmured the other toys. One by one they closed their eyes and fell asleep.

You can imagine Tom and Sarah's surprise the next morning when Mum told them off for leaving every single one of their toys except Jack-in-the-Box scattered all over the playroom. And she wouldn't believe them when they said that they hadn't.